·CULLY·CULLY· ·AND·THE·BEAR·

BY WILSON GAGE

PICTURES BY
JAMES STEVENSON

Greenwillow Books, New York

For Ava —with love

Text copyright © 1983
by Mary Q. Steele
Illustrations copyright © 1983
by James Stevenson

Printed in the
United States of America
First Edition

10 9 8 7 6 5 4 3 2 1

Library of Congress
Cataloging in Publication Data

Steele, Mary Q.
Cully Cully and the bear.
Summary: Cully Cully, the hunter,
is chasing a bear, or is it
the other way around?
[1. Hunting—Fiction.
2. Bears—Fiction]
I. Stevenson, James (date) ill.
II. Title.
PZ7.S8146Cu 1983   [E]   82-11715
ISBN 0-688-01767-3
ISBN 0-688-01769-X (lib. bdg.)

Once there was a hunter named Cully Cully.
He lived in a house made of animal skins and
bark. He had a strong bow and many fine arrows.
He was a good hunter.

One day Cully Cully was lying on the
ground beside his house. He was trying to take a
nap in the sun. He turned this way and that way.
He could not get comfortable.

"Oh boy," said Cully Cully. "This ground
is too hard. I need a bearskin. I will go
hunting and bring home a soft bearskin
to lie on."

Cully Cully got his bow and some arrows.
He went into the woods. He looked this way
and that way, and at last he saw a bear.

Cully Cully aimed with his bow.
He shot an arrow at the bear.
The arrow only nicked the bear's nose.

"By jingo!" thought the bear.
"That hunter has nicked my nose.
It hurts. It hurts lots.
I will teach that hunter a lesson."

"Oh boy," said Cully Cully. "Here comes trouble. I had better run away." Cully Cully ran. The bear ran after him.

"This is a very fast bear," said Cully Cully. "I think he can run faster than I can. I think I will climb a tree and get away from him."

There was a very big tree right ahead. Cully Cully ran around the tree. He was looking for a way to climb up. But he could not find one.

"Oh boy," said Cully Cully. "Here comes
that bear." He ran around the tree again.
The bear was close behind him. Cully Cully
ran faster and faster around the tree.
Pretty soon Cully Cully was chasing the bear.

"By jingo!" thought the bear. "I was chasing this hunter. Now this hunter is chasing me. I had better stop and see what is going on."
    The bear stopped.

Cully Cully did not stop. He was
looking behind him to see if the bear
was getting closer. He was running very
fast. He ran right up the bear's tail.
He ran over his back and
down his nose.

Now he saw the bear just behind him.

"Oh boy," said Cully Cully. "That bear
is even closer than I thought he was.
I had better run faster." He ran and ran.

"By jingo!" thought the bear. "Now
I am chasing that hunter once more.
That's better." He began to run again.

Cully Cully ran around the tree.

The bear ran around the tree.

Soon Cully Cully was chasing the bear again.

"Oh boy," said Cully Cully. "There must be two bears. One is behind me and another one is in front of me. I am too close to this one in front of me. I think I will turn around."

Cully Cully turned around. He began
to run the other way around the tree.
In just a minute Cully Cully and the bear
were almost nose to nose.

"By jingo!" thought the bear. "Here comes that hunter. He is running very fast. He is running away from something that is behind him. He is very scared. That something must be very big. I'll run away too." The bear turned and ran the other way around the tree.

"Oh boy," said Cully Cully. "There are bears all over the place. I had better run faster."

He began to run faster. He almost caught up with the bear.

The bear heard Cully Cully running right behind him.

"By jingo!" thought the bear. "I must run faster. Something is about to catch up with me."

The bear ran faster, but Cully Cully ran faster still.

Cully Cully passed the bear.

The bear tried harder. Soon he passed Cully Cully.

"Oh boy," said Cully Cully. "This bear isn't chasing me. He's running away from those other bears. They must be fierce bears. I'd better run faster." Around and around the tree ran Cully Cully.

Around and around ran the bear.
Sometimes Cully Cully was ahead.
Sometimes the bear was ahead.

Sometimes they whizzed around the tree side by side.

"Oh boy," said Cully Cully. "I am getting tired. I have never run this fast before."

"By jingo!" thought the bear. "My head is going around and around. I am getting dizzy from running so fast around this tree."

The bear got dizzier and dizzier. His feet got all mixed up. He fell to the ground all in a heap.

"By jingo!" thought the bear. "I have fallen down and banged my nose. It hurts a lot. I think I will go home to my den and put some cool mud on my nose." The bear got up and staggered away.

Cully Cully whizzed by.
He saw the bear stumbling away
through the bushes.

"Oh boy," said Cully Cully.
"There goes one bear!"

He ran around the tree again.
Once more he saw the bear walking away.
"Oh boy," said Cully Cully. "There
goes another one!"

He ran around the tree one more time.
This time the bear was gone. Cully Cully
did not see any more bears.
He stopped running.

13025

"Oh boy," said Cully Cully. "Am I tired!
I think I'll go home and take a nap."

Soon he was back at his house.
"Oh boy," said Cully Cully. "This
ground feels so good. It feels so soft.
It feels softer than any bearskin."

And he fell asleep right then and there.